SPHINX FOR
THE MEMORIES

First published in the United States
of America in 1989 by The Mallard Press

Mallard Press and its accompanying design
and logo are trademarks of BDD Promotional
Book Company, Inc.

Produced by
Twin Books
Sherwood Place
Greenwich, CT 06830

ISBN 0-792-45239-9

Printed in Hong Kong

Twin Books

**MALLARD
PRESS**

The Egyptian sun shone brightly as Scrooge McDuck and his charges, Huey, Dewey and Louie, walked along the Cairo street.

"Gosh, Unca Scrooge," said Dewey, "it sure was nice of you to bring us here to see Unca Donald."

"Well, lads," replied Scrooge, "when Donald wrote me that his ship would make a stop here, it occurred to me that he's been away for quite a while. He'll be at sea again soon, so this was the only chance you would have to see him for a long time."

Not far away, Donald Duck was looking through the shops in the bazaar, killing time until he met Scrooge and his nephews. He laughed as he tried on a pharaoh's headdress. "This really suits me," he chuckled.

Two suspicious-looking characters were watching Donald carefully, comparing Donald's image in the mirror with an ancient medallion.

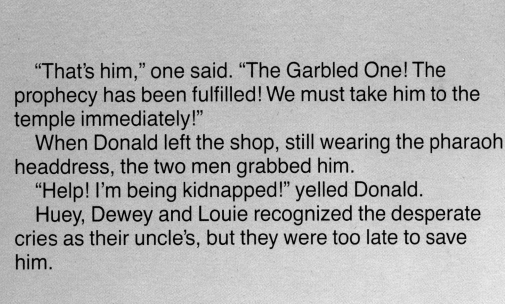

"That's him," one said. "The Garbled One! The prophecy has been fulfilled! We must take him to the temple immediately!"

When Donald left the shop, still wearing the pharaoh headdress, the two men grabbed him.

"Help! I'm being kidnapped!" yelled Donald.

Huey, Dewey and Louie recognized the desperate cries as their uncle's, but they were too late to save him.

Calling for their Uncle Scrooge to come quickly, the three boys followed Donald's captors through the busy, twisting streets of Cairo. By the time they had reached the outskirts of the city, they had almost caught up.

Unfortunately, the kidnappers had camels waiting, and they fled into the desert, carrying off poor Donald.

"We can't follow them without water and supplies, lads," said Scrooge. "Come on! Let's find some camels and a guide."

The two men took Donald to a temple near the pyramids. When they opened the basket, the Princess immediately recognized Donald as The Garbled One.

The High Priest recognized him, too, but he wasn't happy about it. He would have been crowned pharaoh if The Garbled One hadn't returned, and he had no intention of giving up the throne. He would have to think of a way to get rid of Donald.

While the High Priest plotted, The Garbled One's subjects pampered him. He was fed delicious food, fanned by beautiful servants, and given a comfortable place to rest.

Donald was enjoying every minute, even though he had no idea why everyone was being so nice to him.

He found out that night when the Princess came for him. "It's time," she said. "The moon is full, and everyone is waiting for you."

She took Donald into the courtyard and seated him on The Garbled One's throne. Then she said some magic words over an ancient urn.

Suddenly, out of the urn came a spirit that looked just like Donald—it was The Garbled One!

Donald was terrified. Suddenly, he felt strange. The spirit of The Garbled One had entered his body.

Scrooge and the boys arrived just in time to see the spirit take possession of Donald. They were so shocked that they couldn't move, and a temple guard marched them up to the throne.

The pharaoh was furious. He didn't recognize his uncle or his nephews. "Spies!" he raged. "Throw them into the dungeon!"

Meanwhile, the evil high priest had embarked on a plot to overthrow The Garbled One. He was trying to bring an ancient mummy back to life!

"Rise, Ka-Hoo-Fu!" he chanted. "Rise and obey me!"

Suddenly, the mummy case opened, and Ka-Hoo-Fu emerged.

The High Priest laughed. "Yes! Yes!" he crowed. "Again, O Ka-Hoo-Fu, you must remove a threat to my power!"

The mummy growled. He sounded very fierce.

"Go to the pharaoh's bedroom," the High Priest instructed. "There you will find the one I want you to destroy!"

Meanwhile, Scrooge and his nephews were searching frantically for a way out of their dungeon. They tapped at the walls, trying to find a secret passage. No luck.

"We've got to get out of here, lads," said Scrooge. "We have to find a way to free your uncle from the spirit of The Garbled One."

Huey leaned against the door. To his surprise, it swung open. The guard outside was asleep, so they easily made their escape.

Meanwhile, the mummy Ka-Hoo-Fu was scaring Donald half to death.

"N-n-n-nice mummy," Donald stammered. "You wouldn't hurt a pharaoh, would you?"

The mummy just growled, and Donald backed up against the wall.

At that moment, Scrooge and his nephews burst into the room. Grabbing a torch, Scrooge thrust it at the mummy, setting its foot on fire. That allowed Scrooge and Donald to escape.

In the corridor, they met the Princess. She thought that Scrooge was trying to kidnap the pharaoh, and had the guards take them to the courtyard.

No sooner had they arrived than the High Priest and the mummy burst in. "Kill that duck!" the High Priest ordered the mummy.

"What are you doing?" cried the Princess.

"The throne will be mine!" growled the High Priest. "No one will stop me!" The mummy reached for Donald.

Then suddenly, something strange happened. The clouds that had been hiding the full moon cleared, and a beam of light shone down on Donald's head. Everyone watched in amazement as the spirit of The Garbled One began to rise out of Donald.

Then the spirit of Ka-Hoo-Fu rose out of the mummy.

"My old friend," said The Garbled One, "you have been under a curse, too. Well, now the curse is finished," he added. "Come. Let us go to our rest."

And the two spirits disappeared.

"Now what?" said Louie.

"First this miserable High Priest goes to jail," said the Princess. "Then I shall become the ruler of our people."

"Great idea, Princess," said Donald. "I'm not cut out for this pharaoh business, anyway."

Scrooge, Donald and the three boys mounted their camels for the trip back to Cairo, where Donald hurried back aboard his ship.

"It was a short visit, Unca Donald," said Huey, "but it sure wasn't boring."

"No, boys, it wasn't," Donald replied. "It'll be a relief to be just a plain sailor again."

SIR GYRO
GEARLOOSE

Gyro Gearloose had been shut up in his lab for ages, working on an exciting new project.

One morning, he called Huey, Dewey, and Louie over to see it.

"It's fantastic!" said Dewey. "What is it?"

"It's a time machine," answered Gyro. "It can take you back and forth in time. All you have to do is set the time and the date you want."

"Wow! What are we waiting for? Let's try it out!"

"Not so fast," said Gyro. "I haven't tested it yet."

But Huey and his brothers were already pushing buttons on the control panel.

Gyro ran forward to stop them, but tripped and fell against the controls. The machine began to spin madly. When it stopped, the lab was gone. In its place stood an ancient castle.

Two men on horses rode by, chased by a knight in black armor.

"The machine works!" said Gyro. "Come on, boys. Let's give those two some help."

Gyro and the boys made a giant slingshot out of some tubes and an old tire.

"Grab that mop!" ordered Dewey.

They pulled the tire back and fired the mop like an arrow. It hit the knight and knocked him off his horse.

One of the men he'd been chasing rode up and thanked them.

"I'm King Artie," he said, "and this is my wizard and friend, Moorloon the Magician. Welcome to Quackelot. Tonight we'll have a dinner in your honor."

Meanwhile, the Black Knight reported to his boss, Lessdred, the Duke of Northwood.

The Duke was furious. "Fool!" he snarled. "You failed to get rid of Artie, and now we have the magic of those strangers to deal with, as well!"

"They caught me by surprise, my lord. Give me another chance!" begged the knight.

That evening, the knight went to the cave of a fierce dragon. He stood at the entrance throwing stones, and calling him names.

"King Artie says you're so ugly that no knight would want to rescue a beautiful woman from your clutches," said the Black Knight.

The dragon became angry. Flame rose from his throat. He stormed off to hunt for Artie.

43

The King was dining at his castle with Gyro, the nephews and all of the nobles of Quackelot. The dragon stuck his head in a window and roared. His flaming breath almost burned the guests.

"It's the dragon! Save yourselves!" cried Artie, jumping over the table.

Everyone fled in fear.

"We must do something!" said Gyro. "I have an idea!"
He took a barrel of soapy water, made a hose, and, with the nephews' help, sprayed the water down the dragon's throat.
That put his fire out!

Now all the dragon could breathe out was soap bubbles.
"Gyro, that's the second time you've saved my life," said
Artie. "From now on, you will be my wizard and chief adviser."
Moorloon, jealous and hurt, left.
Overnight, Gyro changed. He spent hours practicing with a
sword and lance, hoping to become a knight.

"Why are you doing this?" asked Louie. "We'll be going back to our own time soon."

"Not me. I'm staying," answered Gyro. "I shall be Sir Gyro Gearloose of Quackelot."

The brothers couldn't sleep that night. They had to find a way to change Gyro's mind. Suddenly Dewey said, "Someone else can't sleep!"

Peeking down the hall, they saw Moorloon creeping out of the castle.

"I don't like the look of this," said Louie. "Let's follow."

An hour later, they watched Moorloon meet the Duke of Northwood.

"Help me get rid of that evil stranger," said Moorloon. "His magic is dangerous to all of us." He didn't know that Lessdred planned to get rid of Artie and take over the kingdom.

The Duke listened while Moorloon told him about all of the castle's secret entrances. Then a guard came in with the nephews.

"Take them all to the dungeon," ordered Lessdred, "including this pitiful wizard."

"I don't understand," said Moorloon.

"For some time now, I've wanted to get into the castle to capture Artie, and you have just told me how I can do it!" explained Lessdred.

That night the Duke of Northwood and his soldiers stormed the castle.

Gyro climbed into his armor and joined the battle. Unfortunately, he fell off his horse and was dragged through the middle of the fight, hanging from his stirrup.

The King's faithful troops fought bravely. But little by little they were forced to leave the castle.

"The castle is ours!" cried the Duke of Northwood triumphantly. "And the kingdom is mine," he gloated when he saw that the Black Knight had captured King Artie.

Soon Lessdred was sitting on the throne, wearing Artie's crown.

Meanwhile, Moorloon and the nephews had escaped from the dungeon. The wizard was ashamed of having betrayed his King, and was trying to think of a way to undo what he'd done.

"There's Gyro's horse!" cried Dewey. "Gyro must be nearby. He'll know what to do."

They found Gyro, badly bruised, his armor dented.

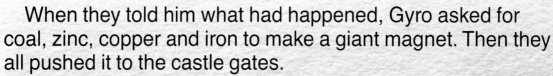

When they told him what had happened, Gyro asked for coal, zinc, copper and iron to make a giant magnet. Then they all pushed it to the castle gates.

"Now we need a storm," said Gyro.

"I can help you there," said Moorloon. He said a magic spell to create a storm, activating the magnet.

Lessdred's men, wearing armor, came flying into the cart, pulled by the magnet's power.

The castle was Artie's once more.

The next day, Gyro and the nephews said good-bye to Artie and Moorloon.

"I'm sorry I tried to take your place," Gyro said to Moorloon. "If it hadn't been for you, my invention wouldn't have worked."

"We'll miss you," Moorloon replied. "Come and see us again."

Gyro set the controls and, once again, the machine spun wildly. Seconds later, they were back in Gyro's lab.

"That was exciting," he said sadly, "but I have to admit life in the days of knights in armor is not for me."

"I'm glad you found that out," said Louie smiling. "Our own time isn't really so bad, is it?"